The Hare-Brained Crocodiles

and other silly stories

Compiled by Vic Parker

Miles Kelly

First published in 2013 by Miles Kelly Publishing Ltd
Harding's Barn, Bardfield End Green, Thaxted, Essex, CM6 3PX, UK

2 4 6 8 10 9 7 5 3 1

Publishing Director Belinda Gallagher
Creative Director Jo Cowan
Editorial Director Rosie McGuire
Senior Editor Carly Blake
Editorial Assistant Amy Johnson
Designer Joe Jones
Production Manager Elizabeth Collins
Reprographics Stephan Davis, Jennifer Hunt, Thom Allaway

ISBN 978-1-84810-929-2

Printed in China

British Library Cataloging-in-Publication Data
A catalog record for this book is available from the British Library

ACKNOWLEDGMENTS
The publishers would like to thank the following artists who have contributed to this book:
Beehive Illustration Agency: Rosie Brooks, Mike Phillips
Jan Lewis (inc. cover), Aimee Mappley (decorative frames)

All other artwork from the Miles Kelly Artwork Bank

Made with paper from a sustainable forest

www.mileskelly.net   info@mileskelly.net

www.factsforprojects.com

Contents

The Farmer and the Money-Lender

By Joseph Jacobs

There was once a farmer who suffered much at the hands of a money-lender. Good harvests or bad, the farmer was always poor, and the money-lender was always rich. At last, when he hadn't a dollar left, the farmer went to the money-lender's house and said, "You can't squeeze water from a stone, and, as you have nothing to get from me now, you might tell me the secret of becoming rich."

"My friend," replied the money-lender knowingly, "riches come from God, or Ram – ask him."

"Thank you, I will!" replied the farmer, so he prepared three cakes to last him on the journey and set out to find Ram.

First he met a priest, or Brahman, and to him he gave a cake, asking him to point out the road that leads to Ram. But the Brahman only took the cake and went on his way without a word.

Next the farmer met a holy man, or Yogi, and to him he gave a cake, without receiving any help in return.

At last he came upon a poor man sitting under a tree, and finding out he was hungry, the kindly farmer gave the poor man his last cake. The farmer sat down to rest beside him, and they entered into conversation.

"Where are you going?" asked the poor man.

"Oh, I have a long journey before me, for I am going to find Ram!" replied the farmer. "I don't suppose you could tell me which way to go?"

"Perhaps I can," said the poor man, smiling, "for *I* am Ram! What do you want of me?"

Then the farmer told him the whole story. Ram, taking pity on him, gave him a conch shell, and showed him how to blow it in a particular way, saying, "Remember! Whatever you wish for, you have only to blow the conch that way and your wish will be fulfilled. Only, be careful of that money-lender, for even magic is not proof against his devious ways!"

The farmer went back to his village rejoicing.

The money-lender noticed his high spirits at once, and said to himself, "Some good fortune must have befallen the stupid fellow to make him hold his head so joyfully." Therefore he went over to the simple farmer's house and congratulated him on his good fortune in such cunning words, pretending to have heard all about what had happened.

Before long the farmer found himself telling the whole story – all except the secret of blowing the conch, for – with all his simplicity – the farmer was not quite such a fool as to tell that.

Nevertheless, the money-lender was determined to have the conch shell by hook or by crook. So he waited for a favorable opportunity and, deviously, stole the conch from the farmer. But, after nearly bursting himself with blowing the conch shell in

every conceivable way, he had no choice but to give up trying. However, being determined to succeed,

he went back to the farmer, and said coolly, "Look here! I've got your conch, but I can't use it. You haven't got it, so it's clear you

9

can't use it either. Business is at a standstill unless we make a bargain. Now, I promise to give you back your conch and never to interfere with your using it, on one condition, which is this – whatever you get from it, I am to get double."

"Never!" cried the farmer. "That would be the old business all over again!"

"Not at all!" replied the cunning money-lender. "You will have your share! Now, don't be miserable, for if you get all you want, what can it matter to you if I am rich or poor?"

At last, though he didn't want to give the money-lender anything, the farmer was forced to give in. From that time, no matter what he gained by the power of the conch, the money-lender gained double. And the knowledge that this was so preyed upon the farmer's mind day and night, so that he had no satisfaction out of anything.

At last there came a very dry season – so dry that the farmer's crops withered for want of rain. Then he blew his conch and wished for a well to water them, and lo! There was the well, but the money-lender had two! Two beautiful new wells!

This was too much for any farmer to stand, and he brooded over it and brooded over it, till at last a bright idea came into his head. The farmer seized the conch, blew it loudly, and cried out, "Oh, Ram! I wish to be blind in one eye!" And so he was, in a twinkling, but the money-lender, of course, was blind in both, and in trying to steer his way between the two new wells he fell into one, and was drowned.

This true story shows that a farmer once got the better of a money-lender – but only by losing one of his eyes.

The Hare-Brained Crocodiles

An extract from *The White Hare and the Crocodiles*
by Yei Theodora Ozaki

Long, long ago, when all the animals could talk, there lived in the province of Inaba in Japan, a little white hare. His home was on the island of Oki, and just across the sea was the mainland of Inaba.

Now the hare was bored with life on the tiny island of Oki and wanted very much to cross over to Inaba, where he had heard there were all sorts of new sights to be seen and adventures to be had. Day after day he would go out and sit on the shore and look longingly over the water in the direction of Inaba, and day after day he hoped to find some way of getting across.

One day as usual, the hare was standing on the beach, looking toward the mainland across the water, when he saw a great crocodile swimming near the island.

'This is lucky!' thought the hare. 'Now I shall be able to get my wish. I will ask the crocodile to carry me across the sea!'

But the hare knew that crocodiles were grumpy and unhelpful – not to mention dangerous – and he was doubtful whether the crocodile would agree to do what wanted. So he thought that instead of asking a favor he would try to get what he wanted by a trick.

So with a loud voice he called to the crocodile, and said, "Oh, Mr. Crocodile, isn't it a lovely day?"

The crocodile had come out all by himself that day to enjoy the bright sunshine. Fortunately for the hare, he was just beginning to feel a bit lonely when the hare's cheerful greeting broke the silence. The crocodile swam nearer the shore, very pleased to hear someone speak.

"I wonder who it was that spoke to me just now! Was it you, Mr. Hare? You must be very lonely all by yourself!"

"Oh, no, I am not at all lonely," said the hare, "but as it was such a fine day I came out here to enjoy myself. Won't you stop and play with me a little while?"

The bored crocodile was delighted at the suggestion. He came out of the sea and sat on the shore, and the two played together for some time. Then the hare said, "Mr. Crocodile, you live in the sea and I live on this island, and we do not often meet, so I know very little about you. Tell me, do you think the number of your company is greater than mine?"

"Of course, there are more crocodiles than hares," answered the crocodile haughtily. "Can you not see that for yourself? You live on this small

island, while I live in the sea, which spreads through all parts of the world. If I call together all the crocodiles who dwell in the sea, you hares will be as nothing compared to us!" The crocodile was very conceited.

The hare, who meant to play a trick on the crocodile, said, "Do you think it possible for you to call up enough crocodiles to form a line from this island across the sea to Inaba?"

The crocodile snorted and answered at once, "Of course it is possible."

"Then do try," said the artful hare, "and I will count the number from here!"

The crocodile was very simple-minded. He hadn't the least idea that the hare intended to play a trick on him, so he agreed to do what the hare asked, and said, "Wait here a little while I go back into the

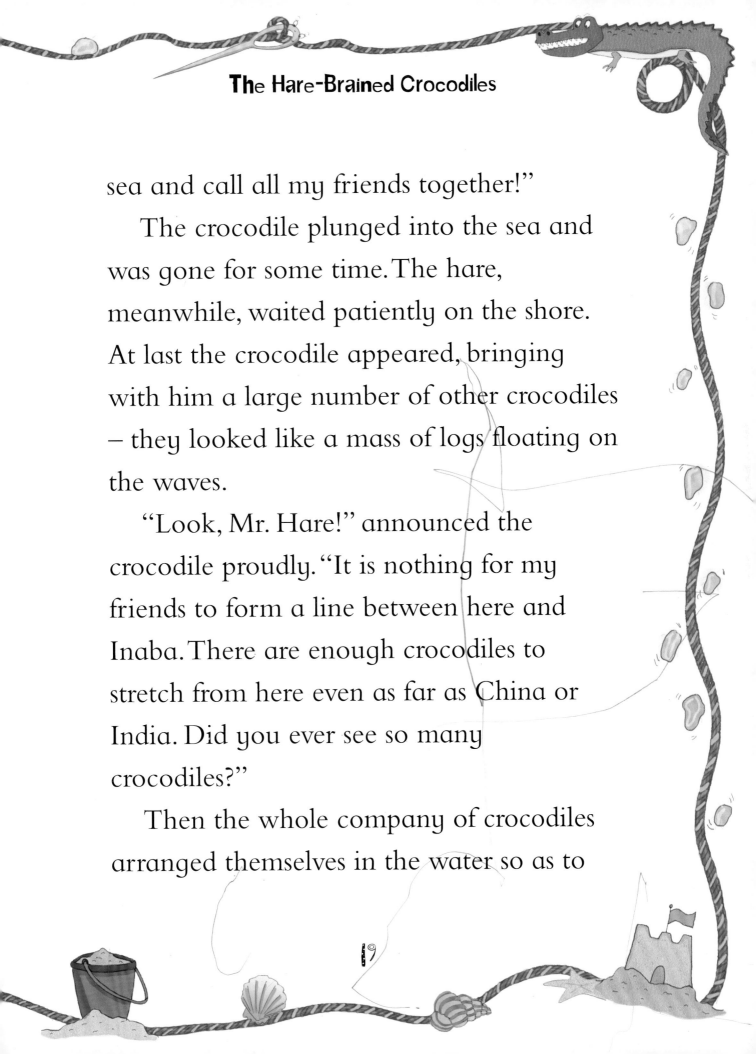

sea and call all my friends together!"

The crocodile plunged into the sea and
was gone for some time. The hare,
meanwhile, waited patiently on the shore.
At last the crocodile appeared, bringing
with him a large number of other crocodiles
– they looked like a mass of logs floating on
the waves.

"Look, Mr. Hare!" announced the
crocodile proudly. "It is nothing for my
friends to form a line between here and
Inaba. There are enough crocodiles to
stretch from here even as far as China or
India. Did you ever see so many
crocodiles?"

Then the whole company of crocodiles
arranged themselves in the water so as to

19

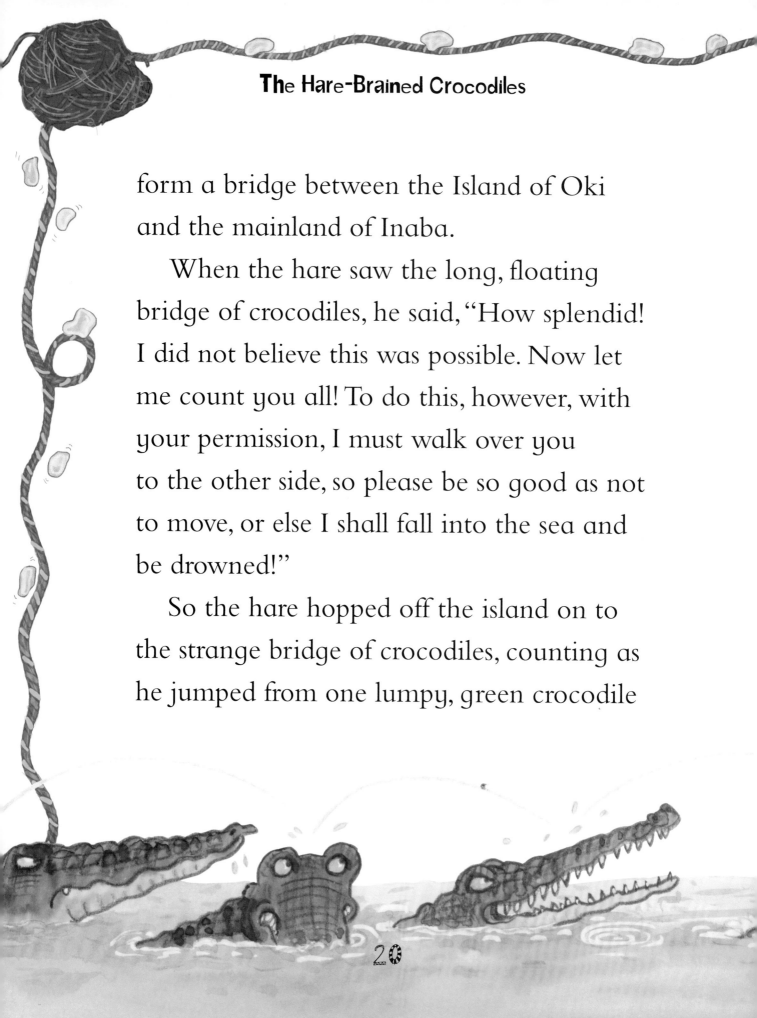

form a bridge between the Island of Oki and the mainland of Inaba.

When the hare saw the long, floating bridge of crocodiles, he said, "How splendid! I did not believe this was possible. Now let me count you all! To do this, however, with your permission, I must walk over you to the other side, so please be so good as not to move, or else I shall fall into the sea and be drowned!"

So the hare hopped off the island on to the strange bridge of crocodiles, counting as he jumped from one lumpy, green crocodile to the next. "Please could you keep quite still, or I shall not be able to count," said the hare. "One, two, three, four, five, six, seven, eight, nine…"

Thus the cunning hare hopped right across the crocodiles to the mainland of Inaba, leaving the foolish creatures red-faced and scowling behind him.

The Darning Needle

By Hans Christian Andersen

There was once a Darning Needle who thought herself so fine, she imagined she was an embroidering needle. "Take care, and mind you hold me tight!" she said to the Fingers that took her out. "Don't let me fall! If I fall on the ground I shall certainly never be found again, for I am so fine!"

"That's as it may be," said the Fingers, and they grasped her round the body.

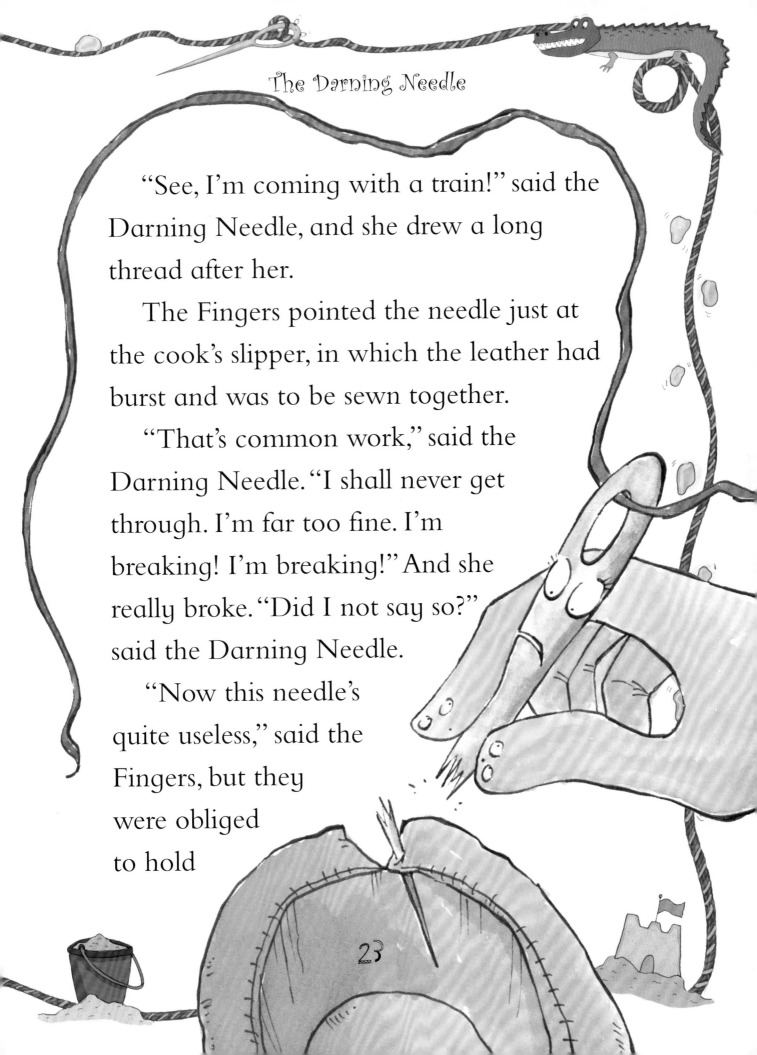

"See, I'm coming with a train!" said the Darning Needle, and she drew a long thread after her.

The Fingers pointed the needle just at the cook's slipper, in which the leather had burst and was to be sewn together.

"That's common work," said the Darning Needle. "I shall never get through. I'm far too fine. I'm breaking! I'm breaking!" And she really broke. "Did I not say so?" said the Darning Needle.

"Now this needle's quite useless," said the Fingers, but they were obliged to hold her all the same, for the cook dropped some sealing wax upon the needle to stick her back together again, and pinned the ends of her neck scarf together with it in front.

"So, now I'm a brooch!" said the Darning Needle. "I knew very well that I should become important!" And she laughed quietly to herself – of course one can never see when a Darning Needle laughs. There she sat, as proud as anything, and looked all about her. In fact, the Darning Needle drew herself up so proudly that she fell out of the neck scarf right into the sink, which the cook was rinsing out.

"Now I'm going on a journey," said the Darning Needle. "If I only don't get lost!"

But of course, she washed down the pipe

and out into the drain and really was lost.

"I'm too fine for this world," she observed, as she lay in the gutter. "But I know who I am, and there's always something in that!"

So the Darning Needle kept her proud behaviour, and did not lose her good humor. Things of many kinds swam over her – chips and straws and pieces of old newspapers.

"Only look how they sail!" said the Darning Needle. "They don't know what is under them! I'm here, I remain firmly here. See, there goes a chip thinking of nothing in the world but of himself – of a chip! There's a straw going by now. How he turns! How he twirls about! Don't think only of yourself, you might easily run up against a stone. There swims a bit of newspaper. What's written upon it has long been forgotten, and yet it gives itself airs. I sit quietly and patiently here. I know who I am, and I shall remain what I am."

One day something lay close beside her that glittered splendidly. The Darning Needle believed that it was a diamond, but it was a bit of broken bottle, and because it

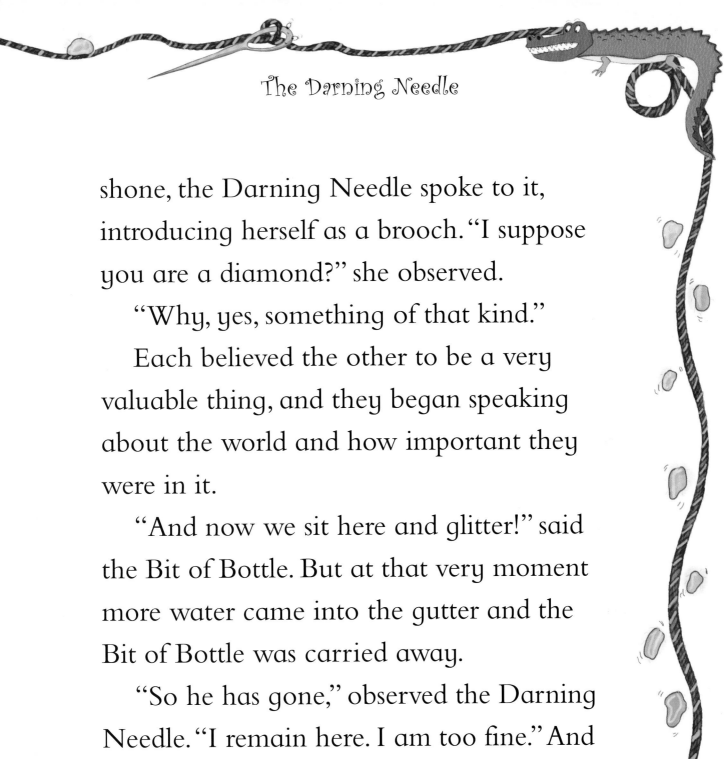

shone, the Darning Needle spoke to it, introducing herself as a brooch. "I suppose you are a diamond?" she observed.

"Why, yes, something of that kind."

Each believed the other to be a very valuable thing, and they began speaking about the world and how important they were in it.

"And now we sit here and glitter!" said the Bit of Bottle. But at that very moment more water came into the gutter and the Bit of Bottle was carried away.

"So he has gone," observed the Darning Needle. "I remain here. I am too fine." And proudly she sat there, and had many great thoughts. "I could almost believe I had been born of a sunbeam, I'm so fine! It really appears as if the sunbeams were always seeking for me under the water."

One day a couple of boys were playing in the gutter, where they sometimes found old nails and similar treasures. It was dirty work, but they took delight in it.

"Oh!" cried one, who had pricked himself with the Darning Needle. "There's a fellow for you!"

"I'm not a fellow, I'm a young lady!" said the Darning Needle.

But nobody listened to her. The sealing wax had come off and she had turned black, but black makes one look slender, and she thought herself finer than ever.

"Here comes an eggshell sailing along!" said the boys, and they stuck the Darning

Needle fast in the eggshell.

"White walls, and black myself! That looks well," remarked the Darning Needle. "Now one can see me. I only hope I shall not be seasick!" But she was not seasick at all. "The finer one is, the more one can bear," she remarked.

Crack! went the eggshell, as a bicycle rode over her.

"Good heavens, how it crushes one!" said the Darning Needle. "I'm getting seasick now – I'm quite sick."

But she was not really sick, though the bicycle went over her – she lay there at full length, and there she may still lie.

Mother Hulda

By the Brothers Grimm

A widow had two daughters – one was pretty and hard-working, the other was ugly and lazy. The pretty, hard-working girl was her stepdaughter, so the woman made her do all the housework. Every day the poor girl had to sit by a well on the high road and spin until her fingers bled.

Now it happened once that as the spindle was bloody, she dipped it into the

well to wash it, but it slipped out of her hand and fell in. Then she began to cry, and ran to her stepmother to tell her of her misfortune. Her stepmother scolded her, and said "As you have let the spindle fall in, you must go and fetch it out again!"

So the girl went back again to the well, not knowing what to do, and in the despair of her heart she jumped down into the well the same way the spindle had gone.

After that she knew nothing. When she came to she was in a

beautiful meadow, and the sun was shining on the flowers that grew around her.

The girl walked on through the meadow until she came to a baker's oven that was full of bread, and the bread called out to her, "Oh, take me out, take me out, or I shall burn. I am baked enough already!" Then she drew near, and with the baker's shovel she took out all the loaves.

Then she went farther on till she came to a tree weighed down with apples, and it called out to her, "Oh, shake me, shake me, all of my apples are ripe!" The girl shook the tree until the apples fell like rain, and when she had gathered them together in a heap she went on farther.

At last she came to a little house. An old

woman was peeping out, but she had such great teeth that the girl was terrified. She was about to run away, when the old woman called her back. "What are you afraid of? Come and live with me. If you do a good job of the housework, things shall go well for you. You must take great pains to make my bed, and shake it up thoroughly, so that the feathers fly about – and then in the world it snows, for I am Mother Hulda."

As the old woman spoke so kindly, the girl took courage, consented, and went to her work. She did everything to the old woman's satisfaction, and shook the bed with such a will that the feathers flew about like snowflakes. And so she led a good life, and never had a cross word.

When she had lived a long time with Mother Hulda, she began to feel sad, but she didn't know why. At last she began to think she must be homesick. Although she was a thousand times better off where she was than at home, still she had a great longing to go back. At last she said to her mistress, "I am homesick, and although I am very well off here, I cannot stay any longer. I must go back to my own home."

Mother Hulda answered, "It pleases me that you should wish to go home, and, as you have served me faithfully, I will send you there!" Mother Hulda took the girl by the hand and led her to a large door. As she stood in the doorway there fell upon her a heavy shower of gold, and the gold hung all

about her so that she was covered with it. "All this is yours, because you have worked so hard," said Mother Hulda, and besides that, she gave the spindle back to the girl – the very same spindle she that had dropped in the well.

When she went through the large door and it closed shut behind her, the girl found herself back in the world again, not far from her stepmother's house. As she walked through the yard, the cockerel perched on the top of the well and cried, "Cock-a-doodle-doo! Our golden girl has come home too!"

Then the girl went in to her stepmother, and as she had returned covered with gold she was well received.

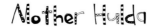

So the girl told her stepmother what had happened to her, and when the stepmother heard how she came to have such great riches she began to wish that her ugly and lazy daughter might have the same good fortune. So she sent her other daughter to sit by the well and spin, and in order to make her spindle bloody she put her hand into the thorn hedge. Then the lazy daughter threw the spindle into the well, and jumped in herself.

She found herself, like her sister, in the beautiful meadow, and followed the same path. When she came to the baker's oven, the bread cried out, "Oh, take me out, take me out, or I shall burn. I am quite done already!"

But the lazy girl answered, "I have no desire to black my hands," and she went on farther.

Soon she came to the apple tree, which called out, "Oh, shake me, shake me, all of my apples are ripe!"

But the girl answered, "That is all very fine, but suppose one of you should fall on my head," and she went on farther.

When the lazy girl came to Mother Hulda's house she did not feel afraid, as she knew beforehand of her great teeth, and began to work for her at once.

The first day the girl went to work, she did everything Mother Hulda told her because of the gold she expected. But the second day she began to be lazy, and the third day still more so, so that she would not even get up in the morning. Neither did she make Mother Hulda's bed right, and did not shake it so that the feathers flew about.

Mother Hulda soon grew tired of her, and gave her a warning. The lazy thing was pleased, and thought that now the shower of gold was coming. Mother Hulda led her to the door, but as she stood in the doorway, instead of the shower of gold, a great kettle full of tar was emptied over her. "That is the reward for your service," said Mother Hulda, and shut the door.

So the lazy girl came home all covered with tar, and the cockerel on the top of the well, seeing her, cried, "Cock-a-doodle-doo! Our dirty girl has come home too!"

And the tar remained sticking to her fast, and never, for as long as she lived, could she get it off.